Mrs. Spitzer's GARDEN

Edith Pattou   illustrated by Tricia Tusa

Harcourt, Inc.

Orlando   Austin   New York   San Diego   London

Text copyright © 2001 by Edith Pattou
Illustrations copyright © 2001 by Tricia Tusa

www.HarcourtBooks.com

Library of Congress Cataloging-in-Publication Data
Pattou, Edith.
Mrs. Spitzer's garden/Edith Pattou; illustrated by Tricia Tusa.
p.   cm.
Summary: With her sure, loving, gardener's touch, Mrs. Spitzer nurtures
the students in her classroom each year.
[1. Teachers—Fiction.   2. Gardening—Fiction.   3. Schools—Fiction.]   I. Tusa, Tricia, ill.   II. Title.
PZ7.P278325Mr   2001
[E]—dc21   99-50906
ISBN 978-0-15-201978-5 hc
ISBN 978-0-15-205802-9 gift edition

First Harcourt gift edition 2007

N M L K J I H G F E

Manufactured in China

The illustrations in this book were done in ink and watercolor on Arches hot press paper.
The endpaper art was done by Rhe Tusa Civitello.
The display type was hand lettered by Judythe Sieck.
The text type was set in Centaur.
Manufactured by South China Printing Company, Ltd., China
Production supervision by Christine Witnik
Designed by Judythe Sieck

Book level 3.0
Points 0.5

46096

DATE DUE

FEB 9 2011	
MAR 3 0 2011	
APR 2 7 2011	
MAY 2 0 2011	
JUN 2 5 2011	
SEP 1 9 2011	

For the real Mrs. Spitzer and her morning kindergarten—
Samantha, Maggie, Lauren, Vita, Sean, Hannah, Jonathan, John, Courtney,
Laura, Dominic, Gabriella, Meilina, Danny, Wes, Andrew, Amy, Claire,
Ericka, Andy, Kylie, and Rudy

—E. P.

For Rhe

—T. T.

Mrs. Spitzer is a teacher. She is in Room 108
of Tremont Elementary School.

Inside Room 108 are six tables—four circles and two rectangles. There is a rug in one corner with real hopscotch squares and checkerboards woven in bright colors. There is also a size chart, a birthday chart, a gerbil in a cage, a housekeeping and dress-up corner, a row of twenty-two pegs for coats and backpacks, and, in another corner, Mrs. Spitzer's desk.

At the end of summer, Mr. Merrick, the principal, walks down the hall to Mrs. Spitzer's room and gives her a packet of seeds.

Mrs. Spitzer consults her calendar and plans her daily schedule.
She checks her tools.

She makes sure the soil is right—light and well-drained, with plenty of room for sprouting. Then Mrs. Spitzer plants the seeds.

She waters them, feeds them,
and makes sure they get plenty of sun.

The seeds begin to sprout.

As the plants grow, Mrs. Spitzer watches them closely.
She checks daily for weeds and pests.

She knows that different plants
need different things.
And that each plant has its own shape.

Some of the plants grow quickly, pushing upward, eager, impatient.
Some grow more slowly, unfolding themselves bit by bit.
Some plants sprout thin and tall.
Some are bushy and wide-spreading.
Some are bold, showy.
They are brightly colored, saying "Look at me!"
Some are silvery and quiet, the color of the earth.

A few are like wildflowers and will grow anywhere you put them.

And some need gentle care, a special watching-over.

As the seasons change, Mrs. Spitzer tends her garden.

And then the year is over, and her job is done.

But the plants will keep growing, uncurling their stems, stretching their leaves outward, and showing their faces to the sun.

Mrs. Spitzer puts away her tools, her daily calendar,
and her plan book. Soon another year will start,
and Mr. Merrick will once again walk down the hall
with a packet of seeds for Mrs. Spitzer.
She will dust off her tools, till the soil.

And a new garden will begin.